A COURT OF THORNS AND ROSES
COLORING BOOK

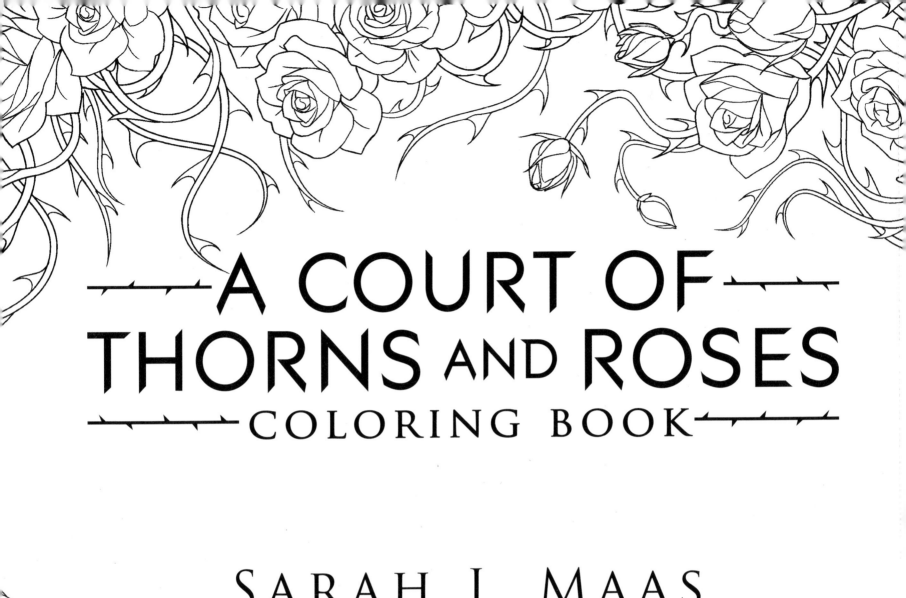

A COURT OF THORNS AND ROSES
COLORING BOOK

SARAH J. MAAS

BLOOMSBURY

NEW YORK   LONDON   OXFORD   NEW DELHI   SYDNEY

I could dry half the meat, and we could immediately eat the rest—stews, pies . . . Her skin could be sold, or perhaps turned into clothing for one of us. I needed new boots, but Elain needed a new cloak, and Nesta was prone to crave anything someone else possessed.

My fingers trembled. So much food—such salvation. I took a steadying breath, double-checking my aim.

But there was a pair of golden eyes shining from the brush adjacent to mine.

—*A Court of Thorns and Roses*

Feyre," my father said. His fingers trembled as he grasped my gloved hands, but his eyes became clearer and bolder than I'd seen them in years. "You were always too good for here, Feyre. Too good for us, too good for everyone." He squeezed my hands. "If you ever escape, ever convince them that you've paid the debt, don't return."

I hadn't expected a heart-wrenching good-bye, but I hadn't imagined *this*, either.

"Don't *ever* come back," my father said, releasing my hands to shake me by the shoulders. "Feyre." He stumbled over my name, his throat bobbing. "You go somewhere new—and you make a name for yourself."

—*A Court of Thorns and Roses*

The estate sprawled across a rolling green land. I'd never seen anything like it; even our former manor couldn't compare.
It was veiled in roses and ivy, with patios and balconies and staircases sprouting from its alabaster sides. The grounds were encased by woods, but stretched so far that I could barely see the distant line of the forest. So much color, so much sunlight and movement and texture . . . I could hardly drink it in fast enough. To paint it would be useless, would never do it justice.

—*A Court of Thorns and Roses*

This beast was not a man, not a lesser faerie. He was one of the High Fae, one of their ruling nobility: beautiful, lethal, and merciless.

He was young—or at least what I could see of his face seemed young. His nose, cheeks, and brows were covered by an exquisite golden mask embedded with emeralds shaped like whorls of leaves. Some absurd High Fae fashion, no doubt. It left only his eyes—looking the same as they had in his beast form, strong jaw, and mouth for me to see, and the latter tightened into a thin line.

—*A Court of Thorns and Roses*

I hadn't known what to expect as I entered the ring of white trees—tall and straight as pillars—but it was not the tall, thin veiled figure in dark tattered robes. Its hunched back facing me, I could count the hard knobs of its spine poking through the thin fabric. Spindly, scabby gray arms clawed at the snare with yellowed, cracked fingernails.

Run, some primal, intrinsically human part of me whispered. Begged. *Run and run and never look back.*

But I kept my arrow loosely nocked. I said quietly, "Are you one of the Suriel?"

—*A Court of Thorns and Roses*

Do you like it?" Tamlin asked quickly. The green of his eyes matched the grass between my fingers, and the amber flecks were like the shafts of sunlight that streamed through the trees. Even his mask, odd and foreign, seemed to fit into the glen—as if this place had been fashioned for him alone. I could picture him here in his beast form, curled up in the grass, dozing.

"What?" I said. I'd forgotten his question.

"Do you like it?" he repeated, and his lips tugged into a smile.

I took an uneven breath and stared at the glen again. "Yes."

—*A Court of Thorns and Roses*

Everything about the stranger radiated sensual grace and ease. High Fae, no doubt. His short black hair gleamed like a raven's feathers, offsetting his pale skin and blue eyes so deep they were violet, even in the firelight. They twinkled with amusement as he beheld me.

For a moment, we said nothing. *Thank you* didn't seem to cover what he'd done for me, but something about the way he stood with absolute stillness, the night seeming to press in closer around him, made me hesitate to speak—made me want to run in the other direction.

—*A Court of Thorns and Roses*

Tamlin smiled at me one last time. "I love you," he said, and stepped away.

I should say it—I should say those words, but they got stuck in my throat, because . . . because of what he had to face, because he might not find me again despite his promise, because . . . because beneath it all, he was an immortal, and I would grow old and die. And maybe he meant it now, and perhaps last night had been as altering for him as it had been for me, but . . . I would not become a burden to him. I would not become another weight pressing upon his shoulders.

So I said nothing as the carriage moved. And I did not look back as we passed through the manor gates and into the forest beyond.

—*A Court of Thorns and Roses*

These bulbs," Elain said, pointing with a gloved hand to a cluster of purple-and-white flowers, "came all the way from the tulip fields of the continent. Father promised that next spring he'll take me to see them. He claims that for mile after mile, there's nothing but these flowers." She patted the rich, dark soil. The little garden beneath the window was hers: every bloom and shrub had been picked and planted by her hand; she would allow no one else to care for it. Even the weeding and watering she did on her own.

—*A Court of Thorns and Roses*

You'll be lucky if she gives you a clean death. You'll be lucky if you even get brought before her." I must have turned pale, because she pursed her lips and patted me on the shoulder. "A few rules to remember, girl," she said, and we both stared at the cave mouth. The darkness reeked from its maw to poison the fresh night air. "Don't drink the wine—it's not like what we had at the Solstice, and will do more harm than good. Don't make deals with anyone unless your life depends on it— and even then, consider whether it's worth it. And most of all: don't trust a soul in there—not even your Tamlin. Your senses are your greatest enemies; they will be waiting to betray you."

—*A Court of Thorns and Roses*

Long, bony fingers wrapped around my arm, and I went rigid.

A pointed, leathery gray face came into view, and its silver fangs glistened as it smiled at me. "Hello," it hissed. "What's something like you doing here?"

I knew that voice. It still haunted my nightmares.

So it was all I could do to keep from screaming as its bat-like ears cocked, and I realized that I stood before the Attor.

—*A Court of Thorns and Roses*

There, lounging on a black throne, was Amarantha.

Though lovely, she wasn't as devastatingly beautiful as I had imagined, wasn't some goddess of darkness and spite. It made her all the more petrifying. Her red-gold hair was neatly braided and woven through her golden crown, the deep color enriching her snow-white skin, which, in turn, set off her ruby lips. But while her ebony eyes shone, there was . . . *something* that sucked at her beauty, some kind of permanent sneer to her features that made her allure seem contrived and cold. To paint her would have driven me to madness.

—*A Court of Thorns and Roses*

The trenches reverberated with the thunderous movements of the worm. I could almost feel its reeking breath upon my half-exposed body, could hear those teeth slashing through the air, closer and closer. Not like this. It couldn't end like this.

I clawed at the mud, twisting, tearing at anything to pull me through.

The worm neared with each of my heartbeats, the smell nearly overpowering my senses.

I ripped away mud, wriggling, kicking, and pushing, sobbing through my gritted teeth. *Not like this.*

—*A Court of Thorns and Roses*

Rhysand stood, running a hand through his short, dark hair. "It's custom in my court for bargains to be permanently marked upon flesh."

I rubbed my left forearm and hand, the entirety of which was now covered in swirls and whorls of black ink. Even my fingers weren't spared, and a large eye was tattooed in the center of my palm. It was feline, and its slitted pupil stared right back at me.

—*A Court of Thorns and Roses*

There was such a thing as Fate—because Fate had made sure I was there to eavesdrop when they'd spoken in private, because Fate had whispered to Tamlin that the cold, contrary girl he'd dragged to his home would be the one to break his spell, because Fate had kept me alive just to get to this point, just to see if I had been listening.

And there he was—my High Lord, my beloved, kneeling before me.

"I love you," I said, and stabbed him.

—*A Court of Thorns and Roses*

This body is different, but this"—I put my hand on my chest, my heart—"this is still human. Maybe it always will be. But it would have been easier to live with it . . ." My throat welled. "Easier to live with what I did if my heart had changed, too. Maybe I wouldn't care so much; maybe I could convince myself their deaths weren't in vain. Maybe immortality will take that away. I can't tell whether I want it to."

Rhysand stared at me for long enough that I faced him. "Be glad of your human heart, Feyre. Pity those who don't feel anything at all."

—*A Court of Thorns and Roses*

Thunder cracked behind me, as if two boulders had been hurled against each other.

People screamed, falling back, a few vanishing outright as darkness erupted.

I whirled, and through the night drifting away like smoke on a wind, I found Rhysand straightening the lapels of his black jacket.

"Hello, Feyre darling," he purred.

—*A Court of Mist and Fury*

Red exploded in my vision, and I couldn't breathe fast enough, couldn't *think* above the roar in my head. One heartbeat, I was staring after him—the next, I had my shoe in a hand.

I hurled it at him with all my strength.

All my considerable, immortal strength.

I barely saw my silk slipper as it flew through the air, fast as a shooting star, so fast that even a High Lord couldn't detect it as it neared—

And slammed into his head.

—*A Court of Mist and Fury*

Feyre," Rhys said smoothly, "meet my cousin, Morrigan. Mor, meet the lovely, charming, and open-minded Feyre."

I debated splashing my tea in his face, but Mor strode toward me. Each step was assured and steady, graceful, and . . . grounded. Merry but alert. Someone who didn't need weapons—or at least bother to sheath them at her side.

—*A Court of Mist and Fury*

The darkness guttered long enough that I could draw breath, that I could see the garden door she walked toward. I opened my mouth, but she peered down at me and said, "Did you think his shield would keep us from you? Rhys shattered it with half a thought."

But I didn't spy Rhys anywhere—not as the darkness swirled back in. I clung to her, trying to breathe, to think.

"You're free," Mor said tightly. "You're free."

Not safe. Not protected.

Free.

—*A Court of Mist and Fury*

The city had been built like a crust atop the rolling, steep hills that flanked the river, the buildings crafted from white marble or warm sandstone. Ships with sails of varying shapes loitered in the river, the white wings of birds shining brightly above them in the midday sun.

No monsters. No darkness. Not a hint of fear, of despair. Untouched.

—*A Court of Mist and Fury*

Both of them were tall, their wings tucked in tight to powerful, muscled bodies covered in plated, dark leather that reminded me of the worn scales of some serpentine beast. Identical long swords were each strapped down the column of their spines—the blades beautiful in their simplicity. Perhaps I needn't have bothered with the fine clothes after all.

The slightly larger of the two, his face masked in shadow, chuckled and said, "Come on, Feyre. We don't bite. Unless you ask us to."

Surprise sparked through me, setting my feet moving.

Rhys slid his hands into his pockets. "The last I heard, Cassian, no one has ever taken you up on that offer."

—*A Court of Mist and Fury*

She took a step closer, sniffing delicately, and though I stood half a foot taller, I'd never felt meeker. But I held my chin up. I didn't know why, but I did.

Amren said, "So there are two of us now."

My brows nudged toward each other.

Amren's lips were a slash of red. "We who were born something else—and found ourselves trapped in new, strange bodies."

—*A Court of Mist and Fury*

A large main room, with a small, shut door in the back. Floor-to-ceiling shelves lined the walls, crammed with bric-a-brac: books, shells, dolls, herbs, pottery, shoes, crystals, more books, jewels . . . From the ceiling and wood rafters hung all manner of chains, dead birds, dresses, ribbons, gnarled bits of wood, strands of pearls . . .

A junk shop—of some immortal hoarder.

And that hoarder . . .

In the gloom of the cottage, there sat a large spinning wheel, cracked and dulled with age.

And before that ancient spinning wheel, her back to me, sat the Weaver.

—*A Court of Mist and Fury*

We seemed to be standing on a landing platform at the base of a tan stone palace, the building itself perched atop a mountain-island in the heart of a half-moon bay. The city spread around and below us, toward that sparkling sea—the buildings all from that stone, or glimmering white material that might have been coral or pearl. Gulls flapped over the many turrets and spires, no clouds above them, nothing on the breeze with them but salty air and the clatter of the city below.

Various bridges connected the bustling island to the larger landmass that circled it on three sides, one of them currently raising itself so a many-masted ship could cruise through. Indeed, there were more ships than I could count—some merchant vessels, some fishing ones, and some, it seemed, ferrying people from the island-city to the mainland, whose sloping shores were crammed full of more buildings, more people.

—*A Court of Mist and Fury*

The people who knew that there was a price, and one worth paying, for that dream. The bastard-born warriors, the Illyrian half-breed, the monster trapped in a beautiful body, the dreamer born into a court of nightmares . . . And the huntress with an artist's soul.

—*A Court of Mist and Fury*

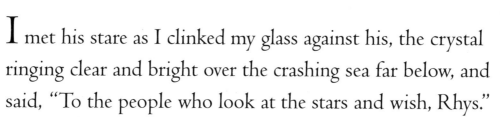

I met his stare as I clinked my glass against his, the crystal ringing clear and bright over the crashing sea far below, and said, "To the people who look at the stars and wish, Rhys."

He picked up his glass, his gaze so piercing that I wondered why I had bothered blushing at all for Tarquin.

Rhys clinked his glass against mine. "To the stars who listen—and the dreams that are answered."

—*A Court of Mist and Fury*

It was not a book—not with paper and leather.

It had been formed of dark metal plates bound on three rings of gold, silver, and bronze, each word carved with painstaking precision, in an alphabet I could not recognize. Yes, it indeed turned out my reading lessons were unnecessary.

—*A Court of Mist and Fury*

Mor led me down the avenue toward another set of stone gates, thrown open at the base of what looked to be a castle *within* the mountain. The official seat of the High Lord of the Night Court.

Great, scaled black beasts were carved into those gates, all coiled together in a nest of claws and fangs, sleeping and fighting, some locked in an endless cycle of devouring each other. Between them flowed vines of jasmine and moonflowers. I could have sworn the beasts seemed to writhe in the silvery glow of the bobbing faelights throughout the mountain-city.

—*A Court of Mist and Fury*

I hadn't even realized what I'd done until his own smile faded, and his mouth parted slightly.

"Smile again," he whispered.

I hadn't smiled for him. Ever. Or laughed. Under the Mountain, I had never grinned, never chuckled. And afterward . . .

And this male before me . . . my friend . . .

For all that he had done, I had never given him either. Even when I had just . . . I had just painted something. On him. For him.

I'd—painted again.

—*A Court of Mist and Fury*

I was going to tell you what I'd decided the moment I saw you on the threshold."

Rhys twisted in his seat toward me. "And now?"

Aware of every breath, every movement, I sat in his lap. His hands gently braced my hips as I studied his face. "And now I want you to know, Rhysand, that I love you. I want you to know . . ." His lips trembled, and I brushed away the tear that escaped down his cheek. "I want you to know," I whispered, "that I am broken and healing, but every piece of my heart belongs to you. And I am honored—*honored* to be your mate."

—*A Court of Mist and Fury*

I angled my dagger over the Attor's bony, elongated rib cage.

"This is for Rhys," I hissed in its pointed ear.

The reverberation of steel on bone barked into my hand.

Silvery blood warmed my fingers. The Attor screamed.

I yanked out my dagger, blood flying up, splattering my face.

"This is for Clare."

I plunged my blade in again, twisting.

—*A Court of Mist and Fury*

The Cauldron was absence and presence. Darkness and . . . whatever the darkness had come from.

But not life. Not joy or light or hope.

It was perhaps the size of a bathtub, forged of dark iron, its three legs—those three legs the king had ransacked those temples to find—crafted like creeping branches covered in thorns.

I had never seen something so hideous—and alluring.

—*A Court of Mist and Fury*

I knew that she was different.

From however Elain had been Made . . . Nesta was different.

Even before she took her first breath, I felt it.

As if the Cauldron in making her . . . had been forced to give more than it wanted. As if Nesta had fought even after she went under, and had decided that if she was to be dragged into hell, she was taking that Cauldron with her.

—*A Court of Mist and Fury*

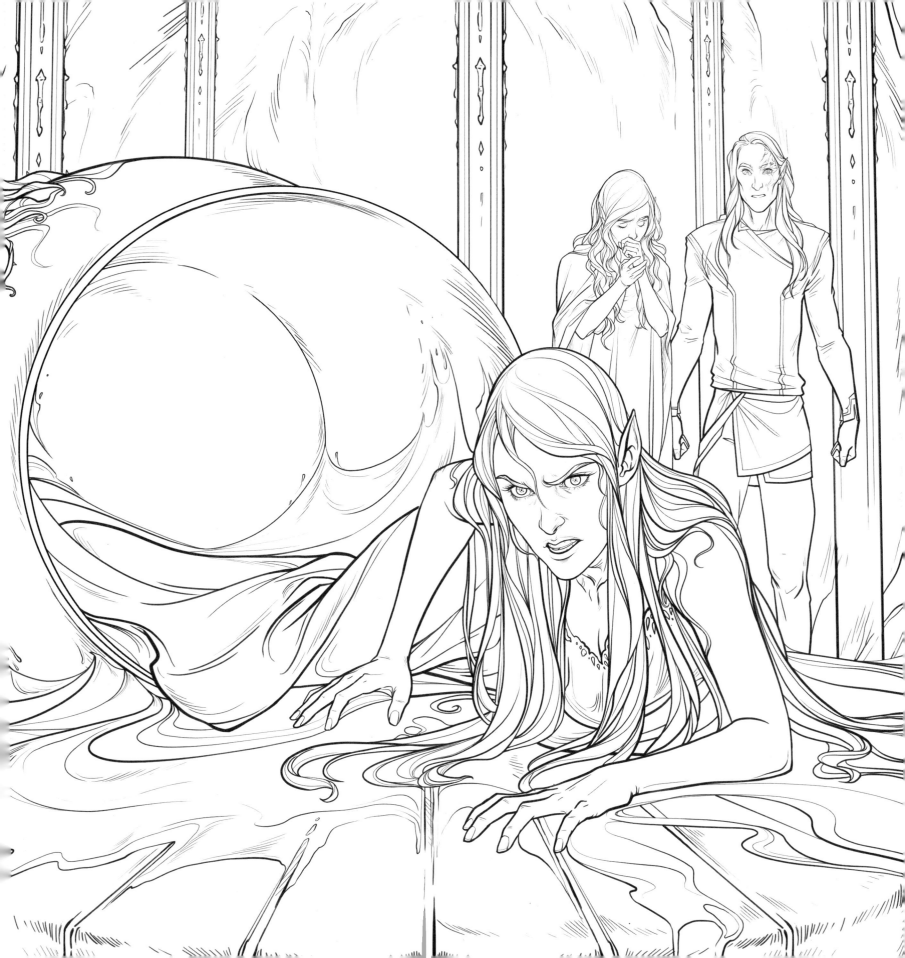

Beyond us, I could feel Ianthe scrambling to regain control, to find some way to spin it.

Perhaps Lucien could, too. For he took my hand, and then knelt upon one knee in the grass, holding my fingers to his brow.

Like stalks of wheat in a wind, the others fell to their knees as well.

For in all of her ceremonies and rituals, never had Ianthe revealed any sign of power or blessing. But Feyre Cursebreaker, who had led Prythian from tyranny and darkness . . .

Blessed. Holy. Undimming before evil.

—*A Court of Wings and Ruin*

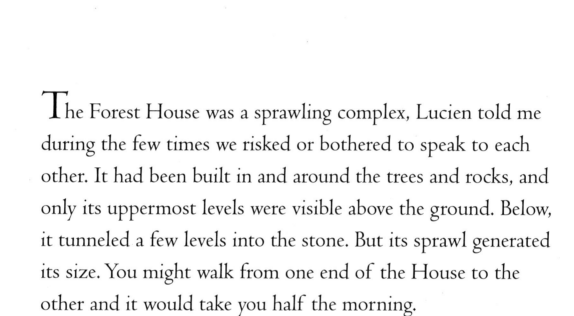

The Forest House was a sprawling complex, Lucien told me during the few times we risked or bothered to speak to each other. It had been built in and around the trees and rocks, and only its uppermost levels were visible above the ground. Below, it tunneled a few levels into the stone. But its sprawl generated its size. You might walk from one end of the House to the other and it would take you half the morning.

—*A Court of Wings and Ruin*

The moment my shoes scuffed against the stone floor, she shot straight up, back going stiff, closing her book. Her gray-blue eyes didn't so much as widen as they beheld me.

As I took in her.

Nesta had been beautiful as a human woman.

As High Fae, she was devastating.

—*A Court of Wings and Ruin*

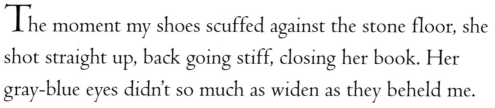

It was as if the base of the mountain had been hollowed out by some massive digging beast, leaving a pit descending into the dark heart of the world. Around that gaping hole, carved into the mountain itself, spiraled level after level of shelves and books and reading areas, leading into the inky black. From what I could see of the various levels as I drifted toward the carved stone railing overlooking the drop, the stacks shot far into the mountain itself, like the spokes of a mighty wheel.

And through it all, fluttering like moth's wings, the rustle of paper and parchment.

—*A Court of Wings and Ruin*

I started at the child's face—what I had not noticed that first time.

It was Rhysand's face. The coloring, the eyes . . . it was my mate's face.

But the Carver's full, wide mouth, curled into that hideous smile . . . That was my mouth. My father's mouth.

The hair on my arms rose. The Carver inclined his head in greeting—in greeting and in confirmation, as if he knew precisely what I realized. Who I had seen and was still seeing.

The High Lord's son. My son. *Our* son. Should we survive long enough to bear him.

—*A Court of Wings and Ruin*

Tarquin ignored Rhysand and me—ignored all of us—as he made vague apologies for the tardiness, blaming it on the attack. Possibly true. Or he'd been deciding up until the last minute whether to come, despite his acceptance of the invitation.

He and Helion were nearly as tense—and only Thesan seemed to be on decent terms with him. Neutral indeed. Kallias had become even colder—distant.

—*A Court of Wings and Ruin*

I kept the crown from yesterday, but swapped my Starfall gown for one of glittering black, the dress made up of solid ebony silk overlaid with shimmering obsidian gossamer. Its skirts flowed behind me, the tight sleeves tapered to points that brushed the center of my hand, looped into place around my middle finger with an attached onyx ring. If I was a fallen star yesterday, today Rhys's mysterious clothier had made me into the Queen of the Night.

—*A Court of Wings and Ruin*

This is Truth-Teller," Azriel told Elain.

Elain's eyes widened at the obsidian-hilted blade in his scarred hand. The runes on the dark scabbard.

"It has never failed me once," the shadowsinger said, the midday sun seeming to be devoured by the dark blade. "Some people say it is magic and will always strike true." He gently took her hand and pressed the hilt of the legendary blade into it. "It will serve you well."

—*A Court of Wings and Ruin*

The ships at the front of the human armada became clear, along with the gold lettering on their sides.

"He named his three personal ships after them," Drakon said with a smile.

And there, sailing at the front . . . I beheld the names of those ships.

The *Feyre.*

The *Elain.*

And leading the charge against Hybern, flying over the waves, unyielding and without an ounce of fear . . .

The *Nesta.*

With my father . . . our father at the helm.

—*A Court of Wings and Ruin*

The Cauldron shattered into three pieces, peeling apart like a blossoming flower—and then she came.

She exploded from that mortal shell, light blinding us. Light and fire.

She was roaring—in victory and rage and pain.

And I could have sworn I saw great, burning wings, each feather a simmering ember, spread wide. Could have sworn a crown of blinding, white light floated just above her flaming hair.

She paused. The thing that was inside Amren paused.

Looked at us—at the battlefield and all of our friends, our family still fighting on it.

As if to say, *I remember you.*

And then she was gone.

—*A Court of Wings and Ruin*

Rhysand traced a line down my spine, then poked two spots along it. "Darling Bryaxis has vanished. Do you know what that means?"

"That I have to go hunt it down and put it back in the library?"

"Oh, you most certainly do."

I twisted in his lap, looping my arms around his neck as I said, "And will you come with me? On this adventure—and all the rest?"

Rhys leaned forward and kissed me. "Always."

—*A Court of Wings and Ruin*

ABOUT THE AUTHOR

SARAH J. MAAS is the #1 *New York Times* and internationally bestselling author of the Court of Thorns and Roses, Crescent City, and Throne of Glass series. Her books have sold millions of copies and are published in thirty-seven languages. Sarah lives with her husband, son, and dog.

www.sarahjmaas.com
facebook.com/theworldofsarahjmaas
instagram.com/therealsjmaas

ABOUT THE ARTISTS

CHARLIE BOWATER was born and raised in the UK. Brought up on nineties cartoons and as much Disney as possible, she now works as a full-time lead concept artist and illustrator. She has worked on a variety of projects, including concept and marketing art for games, editorial work, tutorials, illustrations, and book covers.
She also spends as much time as humanly possible with her nose in a good book.

www.charliebowater.net

ADRIAN DADICH is an illustrator and concept artist from Melbourne, Australia. He has provided the cover illustrations for the Court of Thorns and Roses series.

www.adriandadich.com

YVONNE GILBERT's work runs the gamut and includes children's books, postage stamps, posters, and record sleeves. Her love of fairy tales and history has resulted in her designing and illustrating many books for publishers worldwide. Yvonne lives in Newcastle-Upon-Tyne, England.

www.yvonnegilbert.com

JOHN HOWE was born and raised in British Columbia. He studied at the École des Arts Décoratifs in Strasbourg, France, and now lives and works as an illustrator in Switzerland. John is a renowned fantasy artist and worked as lead concept artist on Peter Jackson's film trilogies, the Lord of the Rings and the Hobbit. John also has a great love for ancient myth, legend, and folktales. And dragons.

www.john-howe.com

CRAIG PHILLIPS has been creating art for books, comics, and advertising for more than fifteen years. His work has appeared in publications for Simon & Schuster, Penguin, Random House, Hardie Grant, Scholastic, Egmont, Bloomsbury, and more.

craigphillips.com.au

BLOOMSBURY PUBLISHING
Bloomsbury Publishing Inc.
1385 Broadway, New York, NY 10018, USA
29 Earlsfort Terrace, Dublin 2, Ireland

BLOOMSBURY, BLOOMSBURY PUBLISHING, and the Diana logo
are trademarks of Bloomsbury Publishing Plc

First published in the United States of America in May 2017 by Bloomsbury Publishing

Bloomsbury books may be purchased for business or promotional use. For information
on bulk purchases please contact Macmillan Corporate and Premium Sales Department at
specialmarkets@macmillan.com

ISBN 978-1-68119-576-6 (paperback)

Illustration credits
Charlie Bowater: pages 27, 33, 35, 37, 39, 47, 55, 57, 63, 65, 71, 73, 77, 81, 83, 85, 87, 91, 93
Adrian Dadich: pages 2, 3
Yvonne Gilbert: pages 11, 15, 17, 19, 21, 23, 41, 43, 49, 67
John Howe: pages 9, 13, 45, 51, 53, 61, 75, 79
Craig Phillips: pages 5, 7, 25, 29, 31, 59, 69, 89

The text in this work originally appeared in *A Court of Thorns and Roses* © 2015, *A Court of Mist and Fury* © 2016,
and *A Court of Wings and Ruin* © 2017, all by Sarah J. Maas and published by Bloomsbury Publishing.

Book design by John Candell
Printed and bound in the U.S.A.
10 9

To find out more about our authors and books visit www.bloomsbury.com and sign up for our
newsletters, including news about Sarah J. Maas.